NO MORE KISSING!

Emma Chichester Clark

A Doubleday Book for Young Readers

for Rodney

A Doubleday Book for Young Readers
Published by
Random House Children's Books
a division of
Random House, Inc.
1540 Broadway
New York, New York 10036

Doubleday and the anchor with dolphin colophon are registered trademarks of
Random House, Inc.

First American edition 2002
First published in Great Britain in 2001 by Andersen Press

Visit us on the Web! www.randomhouse.com/kids
Educators and librarians, for a variety of teaching tools, visit us at www.randomhouse.com/teachers

Cataloging-in-Publication data is available from the Library of Congress.
ISBN: 0-385-74619-9 (trade) — ISBN: 0-385-90843-1 (lib. bdg.)

Manufactured in Italy

January 2002

10 9 8 7 6 5 4 3

It goes on
everywhere,

all over the place,
especially mommies kissing babies.

I wish no one had invented kissing.

NO MORE KISSING!

And I wish no one
would kiss ME,

especially...

people
I don't KNOW!

My family does it too,
all the time.

They kiss Hello,
then they kiss Goodbye.

They kiss Good Morning.

they kiss Good Night.

When my cousin Mimi hurt her finger,
everyone had to kiss it better. She
loves kissing. She'll kiss anything…

...but not ME!
My mom is always telling us to kiss and make up.

Please, Momo

NO WAY!

I've told all my family — my mom, my dad, my grandma, all my cousins, my uncle and my aunts...

But it makes

no difference

at all !

I'm glad I'm not
a baby anymore.

They get more kisses
than anyone.

It doesn't matter whose baby they are, or how much they squeak or squeal...

...or screech, everyone wants to kiss them. So I knew what was going to happen . . .

... when our new baby came.
He screamed his head off.

The more they kissed him,
the more he screamed.
The more he screamed,
the more they kissed him.

"Can't you see he doesn't like it ?"

"Perhaps you'd like to hold him?"
asked my grandma.

First, I showed him my airplane,
but he just cried.

Next, I made funny faces,
but he cried even more.
Then, I juggled some bananas.

He cried and cried and cried.
Now what shall I do? I wondered.
"What's the matter, little brother?"
His eyes popped open.
We looked at each other, eye to eye.

"Little brother," I said, and he smiled.
And then a weird thing happened,
by mistake I think. I kissed him.

It was lucky no one was looking.